Eleven Nature Tales

A Multicultural Journey

Eleven Nature Tales

A Multicultural Journey

by Pleasant DeSpain

Illustrated by Joe Shlichta

August House Publishers, Inc.

LITTLE ROCK

Published 1996 by August House, Inc.,
P.O. Box 3223, Little Rock, Arkansas, 72203,
501-372-5450.

Printed in the United States of America

10 9 8 7 6 5 4 3 2 1 HC
10 9 8 7 6 5 4 3 2 1 PB

LIBRARY OF CONGRESS CATALOGING-IN-PUBLICATION DATA
DeSpain, Pleasant.
Eleven nature tales : a multicultural journey /
by Pleasant DeSpain ; illustrated by Joe Shlichta.
        p.   cm.
Contents: All things are connected (Africa, Zaire)—Sun catcher (Native
Canadian, Algonquin)—Cooking with salt water (Fiji)—The friendship
orchard (Central Asia, Kazakhstan)—Frog swallows ocean (Australia,
Aboriginal)—Rabbit's tail tale (China, Han)—The savage skylark
(Portugal)—Cardinal's red feathers (Native American, Cherokee)—Starfire
(Africa, Zaire)—The grizzly bear feast (Alaska, Tlingit)—Enough is enough
(Native American, Northwest, Quinault)
ISBN 0-87483-447-3 (hc : alk. paper)
ISBN 0-87483-458-9 (pb : alk. paper)
1. Tales. [1. Folklore. 2. Storytelling—Collections.]
I. Shlichta, Joe, ill. II. Title.
PZ8.1.D453El   1996
[398.2]—dc20   95-50387

Executive editor: Liz Parkhurst
Project editor: Rufus Griscom
Cover design: Harvill Ross Studios Ltd.
Cover illustration: Joe Shlichta

The paper used in this publication meets the minimum requirements of
the American National Standard for Information Sciences—Permanence of
Paper for Printed Library Materials, ANSI Z39.48-1984.

AUGUST HOUSE, INC.   PUBLISHERS   LITTLE ROCK

For Michael Storlie—

student, mentor, colleague,
and best of all, friend

The more you know,
the less you need.

—Australian Aboriginal Saying

Acknowledgments

No man (or woman) is an island, especially when completing a book. Heartfelt thanks to:

Storyteller and teacher Kathy Luck, who asked me for a collection of environmental stories.

Seattle storyteller Naomi Baltuck, who told me her favorite nature tales, two of which are included.

Computer genius and friend Tony Earl, who helps me make sense of my software.

Publishers Liz and Ted Parkhurst, who believe in storytelling.

Editor Rufus Griscom, a laser surgeon with a red pen.

Illustrator Joe Shlichta, for enlivening my tales with such skill.

And the good people of the Seattle Public Library, who provided me with a key to the C.K. Poe Fratt Writer's Room, the room in which these tales were written.

Contents

Introduction

The focus of this, my fifth collection of multi-cultural and tellable tales, is the relationship of all things, one to another.

While on an extended journey throughout Mexico in the questing period of my youth, I came upon John Steinbeck's *The Log from the Sea of Cortez.** Steinbeck recorded *The Log* in 1940 while on a research vessel in Baja, Mexico. In the book, a small boy asked him the reason for his trip and what, specifically, he was looking for. After pondering the question Steinbeck wrote, "We search for understanding; we search for that principle which keys us deeply into the

---

*Steinbeck, John. *The Log from the Sea of Cortez* (New York: Viking Press, 1951), p. 110.

pattern of all life; we search for the relations of things, one to another ..."

Folktales excel in demonstrating the linkage of all things natural. They also remind us that the pursuit of such understanding has long been a significant aspect of the evolution of human thought.

The new millennium approaches rapidly. We are faced with a critical question. Are we willing to work together to ensure the survival of the planet as well as each other?

If the answer is yes, we can count on the tales of old to provide ecological explanations, lessons, warnings, and joys.

From the first story, "All Things Are Connected," to the last, "Enough Is Enough," I've attempted to provide a usable collection. It's intended for children, parents, teachers of science, as well as of the arts, and especially for the storyteller, both amateur and professional.

We are all connected by the air that we breathe, the ground upon which we walk, and the stories we share.

Enjoy and use these tales.

—Pleasant DeSpain

All Things Are Connected

Africa (Zaire)

Long ago, a cruel chieftain ruled a remote village in Africa. He was a tyrant who demanded that his orders be obeyed on pain of death. Everyone lived in fear of him but for an elderly grandmother who had lived long and seen much. She was the only person in the village brave enough to tell the chief the truth.

The village was located near a large marsh inhabited by numerous amphibians and insects. The people were sung to sleep each night by the gentle croaking of frogs.

Crribbitt, crribbitt, crribbitt.

One night the chief awoke from a bad dream, and couldn't get back to sleep. *Crribbitt, crribbitt, crribbitt* was all he heard. Because he was in a foul mood, the frog's song wasn't at all soothing. It was most irritating.

Crribbitt, crribbitt, crribbitt.

"Quiet!" cried the chief. "I want all the frogs to stop croaking! I demand silence, and I want it now!"

The frogs weren't used to taking orders from humans, and kept on singing.

Crribbitt, crribbitt, crribbitt.

The frogs kept him awake for the rest of the night, and the chief wanted revenge.

He called the people together early the next morning, and said, "The frogs disobeyed me. Go to the marsh with your sticks and kill them. If I hear the croak of a single frog tonight, I'll turn my revenge upon you."

All the villagers, except for the old grandmother, grabbed their sticks and ran to the marsh.

"Since you are so old and slow, I'll allow you to stay in the village," said the chief.

"And since you are so foolish in your demands, I'll tell you what is true," said the grandmother. "All things are connected."

"What does that mean?" asked the chief.

"You will see," replied the brave woman. "You will soon see."

A strange silence engulfed the village that night. Without the song of the frogs to lull them to sleep, the villagers were restless. The chief, however, slept soundly, and was convinced that he had made the right decision.

Several days later, another sound was heard in the village. *Zzzz, zzzz, zzzz.*

Mosquitoes came in swarms and bit everyone in their sleep. *Zzzz, zzzz, zzzz.*

The chief awoke in anger, batting a thousand mosquitoes away from his head. "Leave me alone!" he cried. "Get out of my house or I'll have you killed, too!"

The mosquitoes answered by buzzing even

louder, and biting him again and again.

ZZZZ, ZZZZ, ZZZZ.

The following morning, the chief told his people to return to the marsh and kill all the mosquitoes. It was an impossible task, however, as there were far too many insects. Without frogs to eat the larvae, the mosquito population rapidly increased. Thousands upon thousands were hatched each day, and now they ruled the marsh and everything nearby. The village swarmed with hungry mosquitoes, and the animals, as well as the people, suffered.

The villagers secretly packed up their belongings and moved far away during the night. Now, the chief had no one to rule over. At last he understood what the old grandmother had meant. All things are connected.

Crribbitt, crribbitt, crribbitt ...

Zzzz, zzzz, zzzz ...

Gulp.

Sun Catcher

Native Canadian (Algonquin)

Long ago, a great hunter named Tcakabesh*
built his lodge on the bank of what is now
called Grand Lake, in Victoria, Quebec.
Tcakabesh was the finest trapper in the land.
He loved to hunt with bow and arrow and fish
with sharp hooks and long lines, but it was as a
trapper that he excelled.

Tcakabesh made snares by twisting hemp
fiber into thin nooses. Sometimes he wove the
strands together to form strong nets. One day,
he made a net as long as an old fir tree grows
high. It was as wide as a summer meadow.

"You could trap a herd of deer with such a
net," said his wife.

*Tcakabesh (Chu-ka-pesh)

"You could catch a family of moose with such a net," said his daughter.

"What *are* you going to catch, Father?" asked his son.

"I don't know," said Tcakabesh. "I'll set the trap and see what happens."

Early the following morning, the hunter draped the net over his shoulders and walked far to the east. He stopped at the place where the sky touches the earth and set the trap with skill. Satisfied with his work, he began the long walk home. The moon ruled the sky by the time he arrived.

Tcakabesh was awakened by his daughter several hours later. "Something is wrong, Father," she said. "It's past the time for sunrise, yet the sky is still dark."

The hunter looked outside the lodge and saw stars shining against the black sky.

"Nonsense," he said. "It's still nighttime. Go back to sleep."

A while later, Tcakabesh's son shook him by the shoulder, saying, "Get up, Father. The sun has not yet risen."

Again, the hunter looked outside and said, "The sun will arrive in the morning. Now let me sleep."

The third time, it was Tcakabesh's wife who awakened him. "The sun should be at its highest point, husband. Yet it is cold and dark."

He looked outside once more. The stars still shone bright. "Something *is* wrong," he agreed. "Get your bow and arrow," he said to his son. "We travel east."

Father and son followed the dark trail back to where the sky touches the earth. An enormous and brilliantly bright creature struggled mightily in the net. But it wasn't a large animal held prisoner, it was the sun!

"Release me, hunter!" cried the sun. "I must rise and light the sky."

"Forgive me, Sun," said Tcakabesh. "The trap wasn't meant for you. I'll cut you loose."

The hunter tried to get close enough to cut the ropes, but the sun's heat was too intense, and he was forced to back away.

The boy attempted to free the sun. He ran toward the burning orb with his knife held high. He too failed.

Tcakabesh called to the forest animals. "I've trapped the sun by mistake. Help me free him so that we may have warmth and light once again."

The animals came forth and tried to free the sun. The deer got close, then had to run back. The bear touched the net with his paw, and was burned in the attempt. The squirrel jumped toward the sun, and immediately jumped back. The heat was overwhelming.

Finally, a brave mouse ran up to the net and quickly nibbled through the ropes with her sharp teeth. The searing heat burned the hair off her back, but she didn't quit until the sun was free.

Rapidly rising into the sky, the sun spread light and warmth throughout the land. All the animals and humans breathed a sigh of relief.

Ever since that time, the sun has stayed away from the place where the sky touches the earth. When asked why, he says, "Because Tcakabesh is too good a trapper."

Ever since that time, the mouse has had short hair on her back. She reminds us that sometimes, when the biggest fail, it is the smallest that succeed.

Cooking with Salt Water

Fiji

L ong, long ago, when the islands were ruled by the great chiefs called Sun and Sea, an old woman named Amara excelled at growing and cooking vegetables. Amara's village was located near the top of a steep volcanic mountain overlooking the ocean. Each day the old woman cooked savory dishes while gazing out upon the blue and green water far, far below.

Old Amara feared the sea. Long before, when she was a child, her warrior father paddled his canoe into a raging storm and never returned. Amara's mother said that Chief Sea swallowed him up because he was angry with her father. Amara kept away from the sea's anger by staying on the mountain her entire life. She

let the braver villagers climb down the steep
path to the ocean shore to catch fat fish and find
valuable shells. The old woman traded her vegetables and cooking skills for a share of the
bounty, and thus she survived.

One day Amara ran out of salt. She made a
sour face and said, "I must have salt for my
cooking pot. Without it, my food tastes as plain
as a banana peel. I'll borrow some from my
neighbor."

Amara's neighbor couldn't help her out,
however, as she, too, was out of salt. Even worse,
there was no salt to be found in the entire village. The salt trader wasn't scheduled to return
to the village for an entire month. The people
complained of their bad fortune.

Old Amara began to think. "A month without salt is a serious matter," she decided. "Chief
Sea has an abundance of salt, more than he
needs. If I cooked my food in sea water, I

wouldn't have to buy salt from the trader. I'd enjoy delicious meals, and be the envy of everyone in the village. I'll have to be brave to face the ocean for the first time. I'll leave early in the morning, before anyone else is up. Cooking with salt water is a wonderful idea! Why didn't I think of it before?"

At dawn's first light, Amara wrapped her largest water gourd in a finely woven coconut fiber net, slung it over her back, and started down the steep mountain trail. It was a long journey for such thin, old legs, and she stopped to rest several times. At last she arrived at the edge of the ocean.

Amara was frightened. Close up, Chief Sea was much larger than she had realized. She tried not to stand too near, but it was high tide, and the cool water lapped at her dusty feet. This, and the soothing sound of the ocean, like a giant seashell pressed to her ear, helped to calm her.

With a shaky voice, Amara said, "I'll fill my gourd, if you don't mind, Chief Sea. I won't take very much. Thank you for your generosity."

She held the empty gourd under water and watched the air bubbles escape. When it was full, she stopped up the hole with banana leaves, and slung the gourd onto her back. It was heavy work for an old woman, but with the aid of a stout walking stick, Amara began the long climb home.

"I hope Chief Sea doesn't miss the salt water I've taken," she said to herself as she climbed. "He has so much and I've taken so little."

Due to the heavy load, the path seemed twice as steep on the way up. Old Amara had to rest after every one hundred steps. At midday she reached a lookout point, halfway up the mountain.

"I've a long way to go, but I'll make it before nightfall. The path is well marked from here to the village. Again, I'll give thanks to Master Sea, and then go home with my prize."

Amara looked out and down at the ocean, and let out a scream! Chief Sea had shrunk! Bare sand was visible for as far as she could see. Trembling with fear, the old woman asked, "What have I done? I took just a little salt water, but much more is gone. Chief Sea will be furious. What will I do? What will I do?"

Having never before left the mountain, the poor woman knew nothing of tides, and how they rise and fall. From the great height of her village, she couldn't tell the difference between a high tide and a low tide. From this vantage point, however, she saw a much smaller sea, and was frightened for her life.

Amara thought for a long moment and said, "I must give it back. Please, Mighty Sea, hold on to your anger. Give me time to climb back down to you, and I'll return what I've taken."

Fueled by fear, Amara quickly struggled down the mountain trail, the heavy gourd bouncing against her bony back. Just as Chief Sun began to set, Amara's feet finally touched the sand. She walked out to the water's edge and emptied the gourd into the sea.

"I didn't mean to take so much, Chief Sea. Please forgive me for my foolishness. I'll go home, now, and never again will I steal from you."

Amara hurried back up the path just as fast as her exhausted legs could carry her. She stopped to rest at the lookout, halfway up the mountain. Again, Amara gazed down at the ocean. The night sky provided just enough light for her to see the water lapping gently up to the beach's highest point. Although she didn't realize it, the tide was in.

The old woman was greatly relieved. "Chief Sea cannot be angry with me now that I've filled him up again. I'll have to cook without salt for the month ahead, just like the other villagers. Such is life."

She continued her journey home in the dark. Never again did Amara venture down to the sea.

The Friendship Orchard

Central Asia (Kazakhstan)

Two elderly friends tilled a small patch of earth on the barren steppe.* They raised vegetables and a few sheep, but life was hard and they earned little. Winter was especially difficult because of the dreaded snowstorms known as *dzhut*,** in which previously thawed snow froze over. Sheep couldn't dig though the ice for food and often perished.

Because they were old and poor, they took care to watch out for one another. One of the men was named Kurai.*** He owned the land on which they lived and worked. The other was

---

* steppe (step) Vast, grassy, treeless plains.
** *dzhut* (djoot)
*** Kurai (Koo-rai)

called Dau,* and he was in charge of the sheep.

One winter, a severe *dzhut* struck their farm. Soon after, all their sheep starved to death.

Dau took Kurai aside and said, "My life has ended. I'll wander into the hills and let the storms take me as well. You've been a fine friend, Kurai. I will miss you."

"No, no, Dau," replied Kurai. "You can't go off and leave me. Who will help with the garden, come spring? Who will tell me stories around the night fire? I want you here, on the land with me. I'm giving you half ownership of the field. You take the lower half, and I'll keep the upper part. The deed is already in your name."

A rare and wonderful thing happened the following spring. Dau was digging in his half of the field and struck something made of metal with his hoe. He dug deeper into the black

---

*Dau (dow)

earth and uncovered a small, iron chest. It was filled with gold coins.

He ran to Kurai, shouting, "You are rich! You can live like a *kahn*.* And you deserve it, Kurai, for you are a good man."

Kurai said, "You found the gold in your half of the field, Dau. The treasure is yours, and yours alone. I'm truly happy for you."

"No, my generous friend," explained Dau. "The gold is yours. You have given me my life. How can I take anything more?"

"God has given *you* the gold," said Kurai. "How can I take from God that which He has given to you?"

"Enough of your stubbornness!" cried Dau. "Take the gold."

"Enough of your nonsense!" replied Kurai. "The gold is yours."

The two friends argued long into the night.

---

kahn (kahn) A tribal ruler.

Neither gave in to the other. They were exhausted by morning and decided to talk with a teacher who lived in the middle of the steppes. He was known as the wisest man in the region.

It took five days to find the wise man's hut. The two friends showed him the gold and told him of their argument. The teacher looked at the coins and then at the men. He looked again at the coins and again at the men. Then he closed his eyes and thought and thought.

After a long while, he opened his eyes and said, "Take the gold to the city and buy the highest quality seeds in the land. Return to your fields and plant the finest orchard in the steppes. Make it an orchard of friendship. Allow the poor to rest in its shade, eat of its fruit, and enjoy its beauty. Rather than divide two friends, let the gold serve many."

Kurai and Dau agreed, and left for the city. They arrived several days later and headed for the marketplace. They searched and searched for a seller of fruit seeds, but had no luck. No one had seeds to sell. The old men were tired and decided to rest for the night and try again the following day.

On the way to an inn, they heard a terrible screeching coming from a thousand caged birds, carried by a caravan of camels. The colorful birds had been captured in the thick forests and high mountains, and were being taken to market. They would be sold as food for wealthy tables.

Kurai looked at Dau and said, "It isn't good to be put in a cage."

Dau looked at Kurai and said, "It isn't right that beautiful birds should be eaten by the rich."

They approached the leader of the caravan and asked the price of the birds.

He looked at their poor clothes and said, "More than you have."

Kurai opened the iron chest. "Release them and the gold is yours," he said.

Dau nodded his head in agreement.

The leader ordered his helpers to set the birds free.

Up into the sky they flew, singing songs of joy!

Kurai and Dau began their long walk home, feeling happy for the birds, but sad for the orchard that would never be. They talked about their long friendship and decided that it was foolish to argue.

Arriving home a few days later, they witnessed a strange sight. A thousand beautiful birds sat in their field and scratched in the dirt. Each held a seed in its beak and dropped it into the loose soil. The dirt was smoothed over the seeds with the beating of strong wings. Then, creating a multicolored cloud of feather and song, the birds rose into the sky and flew away.

Rain fell and the seeds sprouted, climbing slowly from earth toward sky. The orchard took root. Apple trees and pear trees and apricot, too.

Trees take time to grow, and the two old men passed on before they could taste the first of the fruit. Kurai and Dau were not saddened, however, as they had eaten from the fruit of friendship for so many years.

Frog Swallows Ocean

Australia (Aboriginal)

The first people of the Australian Outback say that Bayamey,* Maker of the World, covered the earth with more water than land.

"Hear me, Ocean, and hear me well," said Bayamey. "I have made you the largest, the deepest, and the most powerful force on earth. I love you and all the creatures that swim. I also love the land and all the creatures that crawl, walk, and fly. Take care, Ocean. Stay within your shores. Do not harm the land."

"I hear and obey," said Ocean.

Many years passed, and the land and sea lived in harmony. Some of Ocean's waves felt

---

*Bayamey (Bay-ah-may)

confined in their sea-bed, and wanted to expand, but remembering their promise, stayed put ... until one fateful day.

Wind played hard with Ocean's waves, and they grew taller and taller. It was fun to rise so high and smash on the shore. The waves continued their play and climbed higher and higher upon the land.

Many of the land creatures drowned. Only those who fled to the deepest forests and climbed the highest mountains escaped.

Bayamey was furious with Ocean, and said, "You shall vanish from the earth until I forget my anger."

Bayamey turned himself into a monstrous frog and leaped from the sky down to the earth. Opening his cavernous mouth wide, he began to suck up the sea. He drank and drank until he was full. Bayamey swallowed the ocean and then drank up all the rivers, lakes, and streams.

Satisfied that the earth was dry, he hopped back up into the sky and rested on the moon.

All the creatures of water, air, and land gathered on the dry sand of an empty beach. The fish, amphibians, reptiles, birds, insects, and mammals agreed they would soon perish without water.

"Look up at the moon," squeaked Dolphin. "There sits Bayamey with his lips closed tight. We must find a way to open his mouth. If he opens his mouth, Ocean will return."

"I know how to open a mouth," said Kangaroo. "Make him laugh. It's difficult to laugh with your mouth shut."

"And if Bayamey laughs," said Koala Bear, "he will forget his anger. It's hard to laugh and stay mad."

"Excellent," said Kookooburra Bird. "I'm good at laughing. Let me have a try."

Kookooburra Bird laughed long and loud.

Ha-ha-ha! Ha-ha-ha! Ha-ha-ha!
He laughed all the way to the moon.
The bloated frog didn't grin.
"Let me try," said Turtle. "Everyone laughs when I sing."
Turtle sang a tortured song, causing all the fish and animals to giggle. The moon-frog didn't smile.
"My turn," said Bumble Bee. "Watch—this is funny."
Bumble Bee buzzed Kangaroo's nose, and Kangaroo leaped into the air to escape. Bumble Bee buzzed him again, and Kangaroo leaped even higher. Bumble Bee chased him all over the dry plain. It was fun to watch Kangaroo hopping up and down, frantically trying to escape. Everyone laughed but Bayamey.
"My sister and I want a chance," said long, wiggly Eel. "We are clever dancers; we once made Whale laugh."

All the land and sea creatures were soon amused by Eel Sisters' slippery dance. They undulated up and down, and bobbed and circled and played. They slipped and slid, round and about. They weaved their moves together, looking like two were one. They began to separate for the next part of the dance, but something went terribly wrong. They couldn't part. With all their intricate glides and moves, Eel Sisters had accidentally tied themselves together. They pulled hard, in different directions, and the knot grew tighter. They couldn't get loose and began to argue.

"You're so clumsy!" cried Eel Sister One.

"You pulled too hard," said Eel Sister Two. "You always pull too hard."

"Earthworm wiggles better than you," said the first.

"Mosquito has better moves than you!" yelled the second.

The mammals and birds began to laugh! The reptiles and amphibians began to laugh! The insects and fish began to laugh! All the laughter traveled to the moon.

The great frog couldn't help himself. He too began to laugh. Bayamey opened his mouth wide, and with a roar he let the ocean pour back into her bed. After he spilled the last drops of the ocean, the fresh waters followed. The lakes and rivers and streams filled again.

The land and sea creatures praised Bayamey for his willingness to forgive.

If you look up at the moon on dark nights, you can still see the shape of the frog. It's a reminder for Ocean to stay home in her bed.

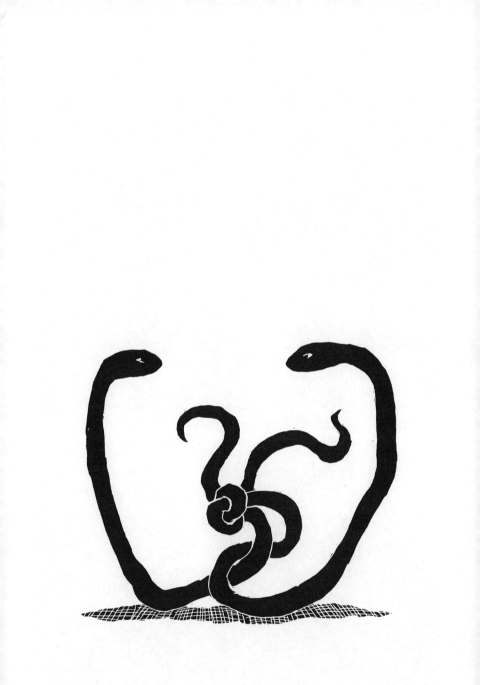

Rabbit's Tail Tale

China (Han)

Long ago in China, animals enjoyed playing tricks on one another. Rabbit was quite clever and usually came out on top. One day, however, something unusual happened ...

Three sister rabbits hopped about in the sunshine on the bank of a shallow yet wide river. They nibbled tall sweet-grass and munched on dandelions, then rested in the shade.

"I hear that the vegetables in Farmer Wu's garden are good and ripe," said the oldest rabbit.

"Unfortunately," said the middle sister, "Farmer Wu's garden is on the other side of the river, and we can't swim."

"There must be some way for us to cross the river," said the youngest.

"Let's touch ears and think as one," said the

oldest sister. "We'll find a way."

The sisters touched the tips of their long white ears together and thought and thought.

Soon, Grandmother Turtle crawled by.

"What are you silly rabbits up to now?" she asked.

Suddenly, an idea jumped into the head of the second-oldest rabbit. "Play along with me," she whispered to her sisters.

"Good afternoon, Grandmother Turtle," she said. "My sisters and I were trying to figure out how many family members we have. There are so *very* many brothers and sisters, aunts and uncles, and nephews and nieces. We are, of course, the largest family in China."

"Don't be foolish," snapped Grandmother Turtle. "Everyone knows that my family is the largest. My children, grandchildren and great-grandchildren are easily twice the number of your entire family."

"Impossible," said the oldest rabbit. "We

demand proof of such a bold claim."

"Yes," agreed the youngest. "Gather your family in the river and let us count them."

"Very well," said Grandmother Turtle. "But you must also call your family together, here on the riverbank. I'll count them. You will lose by a large margin, and that will put an end to your silly bragging."

Grandmother Turtle crawled to the edge of the water and scrambled in. She called to all her family members living up and down the riverbanks.

The second-eldest rabbit explained the rest of the plan to her sisters, and they hopped up and down in glee.

"Marvelous!" yelled the youngest.

"Brilliant!" screamed the oldest.

"Let's get down to the river," said the clever middle sister.

Grandmother Turtle's entire family swam in a slow circle, all around her. The middle of the wide river was covered with turtle shells.

"Everyone's here," sang out Grandmother Turtle. "You can begin counting."

"Not when you're all in a circle," yelled the oldest rabbit. "It's too hard to keep an accurate count. Place yourselves in a straight line from one side of the river to the other. Then you'll be easy to count."

Grandmother agreed, and the turtle family swam into the new position. With their hard shells touching, a perfect bridge was formed from one side of the river to the other. It was just what the rabbit sisters wanted.

One by one the rabbits hopped from turtle shell to shell and skipped across the river, counting as they went.

When all three reached the other side, the middle sister yelled, "You are correct, Grandmother Turtle, you do have the largest family. We, however, are the smartest. Thank you for helping us cross the river. We couldn't have done it without you!"

Furious at being tricked, Grandmother Turtle swam to the far side of the river. She quickly crawled up onto the grassy bank and bit off the rabbit sisters' long, white tails.

"Don't mess with me or my family, ever again," she growled.

That is why, even unto this day, rabbits have short tails. That is also why rabbits are never seen trying to play tricks on turtles.

The Savage Skylark

Portugal

A wealthy landowner and his wife lived in the southern part of Portugal. They had a large house and several barns, and field upon field for growing crops. The husband believed himself superior to his wife in intelligence. The wife knew better.

One day, the wife decided to plant a large vegetable garden and asked her husband to have a nearby field cleared of brush and trees. The landowner sent one of his laborers to do the job. At day's end, the rich man inspected the field and discovered that the work hadn't been accomplished.

He sent for the man and asked, "Why isn't

the field cleared? What did you do all day? What do you have to say for yourself?"

The worker wrung his straw hat in his hands and said, "I tried to do the work, but couldn't. Every time I raised my axe to a tree, I was attacked."

"Attacked by what?" demanded the landowner.

"A skylark," came the sheepish reply.

"The skylark is a small bird," said the land-owner. "The skylark sings when it flies. How could a single, small, singing bird chase you, a grown man, away from your work?"

"But, sir," said the laborer, "this was no ordinary skylark. This bird was ferocious. This bird was savage! She flew all about my head and pecked at my eyes. She wouldn't let me get near the trees."

"What nonsense!" cried the landowner. "I'm sending you and two more men to the field tomorrow. Have it cleared by sundown."

That night, the rich man discussed the situation with his wife.

"My worker is an imbecile," he complained.

"No, husband, he isn't at fault. Keep everyone away from the field for a few days and things will sort themselves out."

"You make little sense, wife," he said. "Problems aren't solved by avoiding them."

"As you wish," replied his wife.

At the end of the following day, the landowner asked the three men assigned to the field to report on their progress.

"We are sorry, sir, but it was impossible to clear the field," explained one of the men. "The skylark is unbelievable! She darted all about us and pecked at our heads. We tried to knock her out of the air with tree branches, but she is too fast and furious. We couldn't drive her away. Please forgive us."

"Forgive you? I should fire you!" responded the rich man. "Tomorrow, I'll send five of my best men to do the job, and the foreman, too. No skylark will stop me from clearing a field!"

That night, he again discussed the problem with his wife.

"I may have to fire the lot of them for incompetence. Imagine, grown men not able to deal with a small bird."

"Leave the field alone for just a few more days, husband. The problem will soon vanish."

"Dear wife, you know little about how to run a farm," he said.

"As you wish," she responded.

At the end of the third day, a nervous foreman reported to the landowner.

"We have failed in the task, sir. The skylark attacked us again and again. We threw rocks and hit at her with shovels and clubs, but she's too fast. I've never before seen such a savage bird."

The rich man angrily dismissed the fore-man. That night, he told his wife that she would have to forget about the new garden patch.

"The bird," he explained warily, "has won."

"Oh, I'll have my garden," she said. "The skylark will be gone in a few days and then we can clear and plant."

"That is wishful thinking," he said. "That bird isn't about to leave us alone."

"As you wish," she said.

A week went by and a strange thing happened. A worker reported that, while working near the garden-field, he saw the skylark fly away. Not only that, but three baby birds flew close behind her.

The landowner immediately sent a crew of men to the field. It was soon cleared and ready for planting vegetable seeds.

That night, he questioned his wife. "How did you know the skylark would leave?"

"It seemed to me, husband, that a creature willing to fight so hard to keep others away had to be protecting her family. It was also reasonable to assume that, once the children were old enough to fly, she would lead them away from such a dangerous place."

"You are wiser than I realized, dear wife."

"As you wish, dear husband," was all she said.

Cardinal's Red Feathers

Native American (Cherokee)

When the earth was young, all the birds and animals were happy.

When the earth was young, all the birds and animals knew how to talk with one another.

When the earth was young, all the birds and animals lived in friendship.

All but one bird, that is. Brown Bird wasn't happy. Brown Bird stumbled with her words. Brown Bird had no friends.

Brown Bird thought she was ugly. The feathers of all the other birds were bright and beautiful in color. Her feathers were the color of mud on a rainy day. Some of the other birds had voices that were lovely and sweet. Her voice was as scratchy as dust when the wind blows. The

other birds flew with swiftness and grace, all about the sky. Wobbling from branch to branch was the best she could manage.

Brown Bird was sad. Perched on a low branch, she watched the other animals and birds.

"Come and play aerial tag with us," cawed Black Crow. "The game is just beginning."

"You could help me feed my babies," sang Mother Robin. Her nest was high in a neighboring tree.

"We are going to bathe in the river," cried Sister Swallows. "Please join us."

Brown Bird shook her head, no. She was too unhappy to do anything but sit on her branch.

Suddenly, Raccoon ran out from the bushes. He was being chased by Coyote. Raccoon zigged each time Coyote zagged and was able to escape. Coyote was tired, and decided to take a

nap in the warm sun. He lay beside the river and began to snore.

Since Coyote often played tricks on others, Raccoon thought it was time to trick Coyote. Raccoon ran from the thick bushes, down to the riverbank. He scooped up a handful of wet mud and glanced up at Brown Bird. He winked with one eye and said, "*Shhh.*"

Raccoon gently rubbed the mud on Coyote's closed eyes.

He winked at Brown Bird again, then ran into the forest.

Brown Bird noticed that some of her sadness had vanished and waited to see what would happen. Coyote slept for a long time. The mud on his eyes dried hard.

At last, Coyote yawned and stretched, then tried to open his eyes. He rubbed them with his paw, and rubbed again. They wouldn't open. He couldn't see. He rolled about on the sand, then stood up and shook himself hard. He still couldn't see.

Brown Bird began to laugh! She laughed long and loud.

"Is that you, Brown Bird?" cried Coyote. "I've never before heard you laugh. What has happened to me? Why am I blind? Tell me what you see."

"I see that you have been tricked, Coyote. I'm in a good mood, so I'll help you out."

She flew down from the branch and gently pecked the hard mud from his eyes.

When he could see again, Coyote said, "You deserve a gift, my friend. I liked your laughter when I was blind. What would make you happy all the time?"

"My feathers are as dull as the mud that closed your eyes. Give me a bright color, one that the other birds will admire."

Coyote led Brown Bird to a shiny rock with

dark, red veins. It was a sacred rock.

"Peck the color from the rock, and I'll paint your feathers," said Coyote.

When Coyote finished painting, Brown Bird was gloriously red! Every feather shone as bright as a flickering fire.

"You are beautiful," said Coyote. "Cardinal is your new name."

The once brown bird, now turned red, was happy at last.

She sang sweet songs, and flew about the sky with speed and grace. She made friends with all the other birds and animals.

This happened long ago, when the earth was young.

Starfire

Africa (Zaire)

Long ago, when the earth was young, humans and animals could talk to one another. Fire did not exist in the early times, and humans often suffered from the cold. Because there was no fire, they couldn't cook their food. Humans wanted fire to make their lives easier. They asked the animals for help.

"You don't need fire," trumpeted Elephant. "Grow your skin thick like mine, and eat only green vegetation. Then you will not suffer."

"Fire isn't necessary," hissed Python. "It's your blood that causes you misery. Human blood is too hot. Make it run cold, like mine, and you'll not notice cold nights."

"Humans need more hair," screeched

Chimpanzee. "Grow hair all over your body, like I do, and you won't be so cold."

"No," cried the humans, "we can't change ourselves into animals. We are the way we are, and we want fire."

Jumping Spider said, "I'll help you. Fire lives far away, but I know just how to reach him."

Jumping Spider spun a long, long silken thread. She made it strong and light. After tying one end to a tree, she called to the wind, "Carry my thread to the sky."

Wind agreed, and blew the other end of the silken thread all the way up to the sky.

"Hurry," Jumping Spider said to Woodpecker. "Follow the thread to the sky. Help the humans. They need fire."

Woodpecker flew along the path of the thread until he reached the end. Then he began to peck at the sky with his sharp and powerful beak.

Rat-a-tat-tat. Rat-a-tat-tat. Rat-a-tat-tat.

Woodpecker pecked several small holes in the sky. Suddenly, bright stars appeared through the holes.

"Look!" cried Jumping Spider from down on the ground. "Star is made of fire. Star, will you give fire to humans?"

"Yes," answered Star, "but only if humans are brave. One will have to climb up here to get it."

The bravest human said, "I'll go."

He climbed Jumping Spider's silk thread, all the way to the sky. He broke off a tiny piece of a star and carried it back to earth.

Ever since that time, humans have had fire. Those who remember the old stories, however, call it Starfire.

The Grizzly Bear Feast

Alaska (Tlingit)

One day long ago, an old hunter of the Raven Clan was lonely. He had lived so long that his family and friends had already passed on. He decided it was time to end his life.

"I have hunted and killed many bears," he said to the wind. "It is right that the bears should feast on me."

Early the next morning, he walked to a river teeming with salmon. The grizzlies came here each day to feed. The old man sat on a large, flat rock next to the river. "This is a good place to die," he said to the wind.

Suddenly, he heard a rustling in the bushes, followed by a loud GROWL! Three enormous grizzlies headed straight for him. He jumped up, and, in spite of himself, yelled, "Wait, don't eat me. I'm here to invite *you* to dinner."

The lead bear, an old male, grunted and sniffed and growled at the other bears to wait.

"I'm a lonely old hunter," said the man, "and before I die, I'd like to make amends. Please come to my home tomorrow, when the sun is highest. I'll prepare a feast. Will you come?"

The lead bear thought for a long moment, then shook his massive head, yes. He grunted to the other bears and they followed him as he turned and walked back into the forest.

"Interesting," said the hunter to the wind. "I thought I was going to be dinner for the enemy. Instead, I'm hosting the enemies' dinner."

He went home and began the preparations. He cleaned his clothes and swept out his lodge. He washed his cooking utensils and chopped a large pile of firewood. Then he gathered enough food to feed the entire village.

"Why are you doing this?" asked several of his clan. "Who are you entertaining?"

"Grizzlies," he answered.

The villagers decided that old age had taken his mind, and left him alone.

All was ready the following morning. The hunter painted red stripes on his arms and chest to mark the celebration, and waited until the sun rose to its zenith.

The bears splashed through a nearby creek and walked boldly into the village. The people were frightened and ran into their houses. The hunter stood at his door with his arms open wide.

"Welcome, my friends," he said. "Sit here, in the shade of my lodge. I hope your bellies are empty, as I've prepared a feast."

Grunting approval, the lead bear shuffled over to the seat of honor and sat on the hunter's finest blanket. The two younger bears sat on the ground nearby.

The old man served salmon and fresh blueberries, picked that morning. He also offered a large tray of preserved cranberries. The bears ate and enjoyed everything, then sat contentedly with the old man as he smoked his pipe of peace. After smoking, the hunter told tales of his greatest adventures. The bears listened politely. When he finished, he asked the lead bear to share a story. Gesturing wildly with paws and claws, the grizzly grunted, huffed, and growled for more than an hour. His tale required many details.

The man couldn't understand anything the bear said, but he proved a good host and listened well.

The feast ended and each bear licked the paint off the man's chest and arms. It was their way of saying goodbye.

That night the hunter dreamed of the lead bear. The bear spoke to him in the language of humans.

"Thank you for your kindness, old man. I, too, have lived long, and lost many friends and family members. I know the cold feeling of loneliness. Consider me your friend. When you grow sad, remember that you are alone no longer."

The man remembered and was grateful.

The villagers were impressed with the bears' visit, and decided that it is good to invite an enemy to a feast. It's even better to turn an enemy into a friend.

Enough Is Enough

Native American (Northwest: Quinault)

In the time of the ancients, peace ruled the land. The plants, animals, and people lived together in harmony. Always, there was an abundance of food, water, and shelter. This was in the beginning time. This was in the time of satisfaction.

Long ago, people lived on the flat plains that are now called the eastern part of Washington state. A mighty mountain range separates the state's east side from the west, or ocean side. This was not true in the beginning.

Rain did not fall from the clouds in the beginning time. Great Spirit made moisture flow up from the earth. Trees, streams, and grassy fields drank from below ground. Always, there was moisture.

Until one day ... the waters below the earth dried up. Trees and grasses turned brown, then black. The waters in the rivers and streams evaporated. The salmon couldn't swim in air. The drinking holes for the animals and humans vanished. Many birds, deer, skunk, and bear perished. The ancient people suffered great thirst. Many died.

A brave warrior walked far to the West to talk with Ocean.

"Without water, everything dies. Help us to live."

Ocean said, "I will send you some of my sons, called Clouds. I will send you some of my daughters, called Rain."

Clouds and Rain flew to the parched, eastern lands and gave of their water. The grasses turned green. The streams and rivers filled. The salmon flourished. The animals drank. The people rejoiced and made a plan.

"We'll dig a large hole in the earth," they said.

"We'll ask Clouds and Rain to fill the hole," they said.

"We'll always have enough water. Never again will we run dry," they said.

The yellow moon became full and round many times before the enormous pit was dug. Ocean grew lonely for his children. He sent a messenger to the people and asked them to send Clouds and Rain back home.

"No," said the people. "We must have more water."

"You have an abundance of moisture," said the messenger. "Ocean and his children have been generous. You have what you need. Let that be enough."

"No," answered the people. "We want more."

"You will anger Ocean," cried the messenger.

"We will not release Ocean's children," said the people.

"Enough is enough," replied the messenger.

The messenger returned to Ocean without Clouds. The messenger returned to Ocean without Rain.

Ocean was angry, and spoke with Great Spirit. "The people are filled with greed. They are not satisfied when they have enough. They always want more. They want too much."

Great Spirit decided to punish the people. He reached down and scooped up an enormous mound of earth from the West, and set it down across the flat plains of the East. The new mountainous wall separated the wet part of the land from the dry region. That wall is now called the Cascade Range. Ocean filled in the crater left empty on the west side. That is now called Puget Sound.

The ancient people kept Ocean's sons and

daughters on the east side of the Cascades. Clouds and Rain filled the large pit dug by the eastern dwellers. It is called Lake Chelan, and is still used to store water. The plains remain dry, however, as Clouds and Rain are unhappy, and give little of their moisture. They miss their father and wish to return home.

Ocean grieves for his children, as well. He calls to them night and day. You can hear his sad song in the lapping of the waves against the shore.

Notes

Motifs given are from Margaret Read MacDonald, *The Storyteller's Sourcebook: A Subject, Title, and Motif-Index to Folklore Collections for Children* (Detroit: Gale/Neal-Schuman, 1982).

The stories in this collection are retellings of traditional folktales. Each contains original imagery, pacing, and most significantly, an original narrative voice that can only be achieved through years of telling it aloud, prior to writing it down.

All Things Are Connected

Africa (Zaire), page 13

Motif J10, *Wisdom (knowledge) acquired from experience.*

I first heard this story from Seattle storyteller Naomi Baltuck. She loves it not only for its meaning, but for the inherent opportunities for audience participation. Use the sounds made by the frogs and mosquitoes as well as the refrain, "All things are connected."

For another version see *The Crest and the Hide* by Harold Courlander (New York: Coward, McCann and Geoghehan, 1982), pp. 103-4.

A story from the Philippines makes the same point but

with a slightly different plot. See *I Saw a Rocket Walk a Mile* by Carl Withers (New York: Holt, Rinehart and Winston, 1965), pp. 131-32.

Sun Catcher

Native Canadian (Algonquin), page 19

Motif A728.2.1, *Sun is caught in snare. Beaver gnaws sun free.*

A popular myth worldwide, "Sun Catcher" has several variants featuring other animals freeing the sun. Beaver, Squirrel, and Mouse are the most popular.

This version is based on a story recorded in the early 1600s by the Jesuits living with the Algonquins near Lake Huron. See *The Man in the Moon: Sky Tales from Many Lands* by Alta Jablow and Carl Withers (New York: Holt, Rinehart & Winston, 1969), pp. 79-80.

Cooking with Salt Water

Fiji, page 25

Motif J1959.3, *Woman thinks tides recede because she dips in water.*

The successful telling of this tale depends upon portraying Amara as a believable character. Enact her fear, bravery, hope, surprise, defeat, and relief, with compassion as well as fun.

I initially heard it told by a Fijian student named Amara who was attending The College of the Virgin Islands during the summer of 1967. I taught my class on the beach the day we shared folktales, and Amara earned an *A* for such an appropriate choice. She explained that she heard the story from her mother.

For another version see *The Magic Banana and Other Polynesian Tales* by Erick Berry (New York: John Day Company, 1958), pp. 50-55.

The Friendship Orchard
Central Asia (Kazakhstan), page 33

Motif W11.17, *Two generous friends.*

Kazakhs were an independent and nomadic tribe until defeated by the Russians in the mid-nineteenth century. Their stories often demonstrate pride in friendship and the desire for an easier life.

Twenty years of telling have produced a nearly original version of this tale. At its heart, however, it remains pure. I discovered it in *Stories of the Steppes: Kazakh Folktales* by Mary Lou Masey (New York: David McKay Company, 1968), pp. 50-61.

Frog Swallows Ocean
Australia (Aboriginal), page 41

Motif A751.3.1.3, *Frog swallows ocean.*

Loosen up and undulate your head, neck, and arms to imitate the eel sisters' dance. The objective is to move your listeners from grins to laughter.

Francis Carpenter discovered this tale in *The Land of the Kangaroo* (London: Thomas W. Knox, 1896).

She collected it in *Wonder Tales of Seas and Ships* (New York: Doubleday & Co., 1959), pp. 29-36.

An interesting variation, in which the man in the moon is a frog, comes from Native Americans in British Columbia (Lillooet). See *How the People Sang the Mountains Up: How and Why Stories* by Maria Leach (New York: Viking, 1967), pp. 31-33.

Rabbit's Tail Tale

China (Han), page 49

Motif K579.2.2, *Hare crosses to mainland by counting crocodiles. Tail bitten off in revenge.*

The Han people make up the largest population in China (over ninety percent) and tell tales that originated more than two thousand years ago. The turtle family represents the great pride the Chinese held for large families prior to the twentieth century. Japanese variants of this tale involve crocodiles.

See *The Magic Boat and Other Chinese Folk Stories* by M.A. Jagendorf and Virginia Weng (New York: The Vanguard Press, 1980), pp. 33-34.

A Japanese version is found in *Favorite Stories Old and New* by Sidonie Gruenberg (New York: Doubleday, 1942, 1955), pp. 347-48.

The Savage Skylark

Portugal, page 55

Motif U120, *Nature will show itself.*
Folktales worldwide abundantly demonstrate that
courage is vital to survival in nature.

I was asked to teach a storytelling workshop at a convention of professional women held in Seattle, during the mid-1970s. My search for a strong and "real" woman-story led me to a collection of Portuguese folktales, which contains the basic story told here. My slant and the need, however, was to make her stronger than in the original telling and yet remain true to the Portuguese version. I find that audiences consistently approve of this one. Share this story with women's groups and watch heads nod with approval over the wife's innate wisdom.

See *Folk Tales from Portugal* by Alan S. Feinstein (New York: A.S. Barnes and Co., 1972), pp. 75-78.

Cardinal's Red Feathers

Native American (Cherokee), page 63

Motif A2411.2.1.13.1, *Color of red-bird.*
The Cherokee, relatives of the Iroquois, made their home in Tennessee and North Carolina. Many of their legends explain natural phenomena with an imaginative logic that not only seems reasonable but makes for good stories.

Two other sources for this tale are *Cherokee Animal Tales* by George P. Scheer (New York: Holiday, 1968) pp. 62-

68; and *The Long-Tailed Bear and Other Indian Legends* by Natalia M. Belting (Indianapolis: Bobbs-Merrill Co., 1961), pp. 62-66.

Starfire

Africa (Zaire), page 69

Motif A1414.7.5, *Star as fire.*

I love the simplicity and grace of this tale of origin and often place it at the beginning of a nature-based program.

Fire originating from the sky is an ancient motif. One of the earliest is the Greek myth of Prometheus, found in *Favorite Stories Old and New* by Sidonie M. Gruenberg (New York: Doubleday, 1942, 1955), pp. 411-12.

An even briefer version of "Starfire" is called "The Gift from a Star" and is found in *Long Ago When the Earth Was Flat: Three Tales from Africa* by Paola Caboara Luzzatto (New York: Collins, 1979), pp. 36-43.

The Grizzly Bear Feast

Alaska (Tlingit), page 73

Motif A1598.1, *Origin of custom of inviting strangers to share feast.*

The Arts Commission of Fairbanks, Alaska, invited me to be in residence during an exceptionally cold week in February, 1978. After an evening library program, I was introduced to a Tlingit husband and wife, who told me this story.

It's also known as "The Cranberry Feast" and is found

in *The Magic Calabash: Folk Tales from America's Islands and Alaska* edited by Jean Cothran (New York: David McKay Company, 1956), pp. 8-12.

Ms. Cothran explains that her version is a retelling of "The Man Who Entertained the Bears," *Tlingit Myths and Texts* recorded by John R. Swanton, printed in Bulletin #39, Bureau of American Ethnology, The Smithsonian Institution.

Enough Is Enough

Native American (Northwest: Quinault), page 79

Motif A900, *Topographical features of the earth.*

The Cascade Mountain Range is seven hundred miles long and extends south from British Columbia, Canada, through Washington and Oregon, and into northern California. The volcanic Mount Rainier, Mount St. Helen's (Washington state), Mount Hood (Oregon), and Mount Shasta (California) are part of the range.

Eastern Washington's Lake Chelan is fjordlike and consists of 61,822 acres.

An excellent story for environmental classes and conferences, this legend easily transcends its regional roots.

I discovered it in *Indian Legends of the Pacific Northwest* by Ella Elizabeth Clark (Berkeley: University of California Press, 1953), pp. 25-26. She explains that Clarence Pickernell, a Quinault-Chehalis-Cowlitz from Tahola, Washington, told it in 1951. He learned it from his great-grandmother.

Storytellers on tape
from August House Publishers

Multicultural Tales to Tell
From veteran storyteller Pleasant DeSpain, twenty "retellable" folktales from
around the world (from the book *Thirty-Three Multicultural Tales to Tell*).
2 cassettes, 102 minutes, 0-87483-345-0, $18.00

Eleven Turtle Tales
A multicultural resource by Pleasant DeSpain, with stories from the Congo, India,
Ghana, Japan, Australia, Panama, Nigeria, South Africa, and Native America
(from the book *Eleven Turtle Tales*).
1 cassette, 56 minutes, ISBN 0-87483-425-2, $12.00

Listening for the Crack of Dawn
Master storyteller Donald Davis recalls the Appalachia of the '50s and '60s
"His stories often left listeners limp with laughter at the same time they struggled
with a lump in the throat."—Wilma Dykeman, *New York Times*
2 cassettes, 120 minutes, ISBN 0-87483-147-4, $18.00

Favorite Scary Stories of American Children
A culturally diverse collection of shivery tales gathered from kids themselves.
Collected and told by Richard and Judy Dockrey Young.
2 cassettes, 60 minutes each
Part 1 (for ages 5-8): ISBN 0-87483-148-2, $12.00
Part 2 (for ages 7-10): ISBN 0-87483-175-X, $12.00

Johnny Appleseed, Gentle Hero
Marc Joel Levitt's stories of the American legend Johnny Appleseed keep
history alive and teach humanitarian values to children.
1 cassette, 45 minutes, ISBN 0-87483-176-8, $12.00

Ghost Stories from the American Southwest
Shivery tales collected from people throughout the Southwest. Performed by
extraordinary storytellers Richard and Judy Dockrey Young.
1 cassette, 60 minutes, ISBN 0-87483-149-0, $12.00

August House Publishers
P.O.Box 3223, Little Rock, Arkansas 72203
1-800-284-8784

*Other books of interest
from August House Publishers, Inc.*

Eleven Turtle Tales
Pleasant DeSpain
Adventure stories for young readers—
perfect for read-aloud
ISBN 0-87483-388-4, HB, $12.95
(Audio available: ISBN 0-87483-425-2, $12.00)

Once Upon a Galaxy
Josepha Sherman
The ancient stories that inspired Star Wars, Superman,
and other popular fantasies
ISBN 0-87483-387-6, TPB, $14.95
ISBN 0-87483-386-8, HB, $24.95

The Storyteller's Start-Up Book
Margaret Read MacDonald
Finding, learning, performing, and using folktales
ISBN 0-87483-305-1, TPB, $16.95
ISBN 0-87483-304-3, HB, 26.95

The Storytelling Coach
Doug Lipman
Principles for giving and receiving good help—on the
stage, in the classroom, in the boardroom
ISBN 0-87483-434-1, TPB, $14.95
ISBN 0-87483-435-X, HB, 24.95

August House Publishers
P.O.Box 3223, Little Rock, Arkansas 72203
1-800-284-8784